Our Little Roumanian Cousin

Clara Vostrovsky Winlow

Our Little Roumanian Cousin

CHAPTER I

THE DOCTOR PRESCRIBES

Jonitza lay sprawled out on the warm carpet in the living-room near a big brick stove that reached almost to the ceiling. Beside him were his playthings and two picture books with fancy covers, but he kicked his slippered feet discontentedly at them, until his mother, seated at the other end of the room, arose, put down her sewing, and with a scarcely audible sigh, picked them up and laid them on the table.

Jonitza paid no attention. Ever since he had been seriously ill the month before, he had grown accustomed to having people wait on him. He now turned on his back and began tracing in the air with his finger the pretty stenciled patterns that covered the walls. Tiring of that, he started beating a monotonous tattoo with one foot, until his mother, with the faintest shade of impatience, said: "I think you'd better get up. You've been lying on the floor for a whole hour doing nothing."

Jonitza arose languidly, stretched himself, and walking over to one of the big double windows, plumped himself down into a deep arm chair in front of it.

Jonitza's home was a very comfortable one-story house in the city of Galatz, one of the leading ports on the Danube River, near the border line between Moldavia and Wallachia, the two provinces which with Dobrudja, make up the kingdom of Roumania. It was in one of the best residence districts, at one end of a high earth cliff. Somewhat below this cliff extended the flat level of the Lower Town, made up principally of mills and business houses, immense warehouses for grain, much of which is exported from Roumania, and wharves stretching out to the river.

The little boy could not see much of this, but far below, in between the scattered apricot-trees and lilac bushes in the garden, he could just get a glimpse of an interesting procession of rude carts to which bullocks or buffaloes were harnessed, toiling slowly upward on a wide road. He had become so interested in the struggles of one cart that looked as if it were loaded with the enormous reeds that are used for fuel by the poorer people of Galatz that he did not hear the bell ring and so was quite unprepared to have a hand suddenly laid on his shoulder and to look up into the smiling face of the family Doctor.

Jonitza had a guilty feeling without knowing why and tried his best to scowl and look away. It wasn't easy though.

"Why aren't you out-of-doors?" the Doctor asked in a surprised tone.

It was Jonitza's turn to be surprised. "Why," he stammered, "it's — too cold," here he shivered, "I — I — I am not well enough."

"What nonsense!" the Doctor said. "The air is delightful. I've been traveling around half the day in it. And, even granting that you're not well — why, fresh air is the only thing that will make you well."

Jonitza suppressed a yawn and looked listlessly about him. The Doctor shrugged his shoulders as he said: "I see I must leave a new prescription for you." Saying this, he tore a leaf from his note-book, hastily wrote something on it, folded it, and handed it to Jonitza's mother who stood near by, with: "Please treat what is written here seriously, Mrs. Popescu. I shall have more to say regarding it to your husband. Now I must hurry away."

But Mrs. Popescu barred the entrance.

"Not until you have had some coffee," she said. At the same moment, a maid entered with a tray on which were coffee and sweets, the refreshments usually handed to visitors in Roumania. The Doctor took a taste of the coffee and one of the sweetmeats and laughingly remarked as he left: "It's only fresh air that keeps me from breaking down under the régime to which I am subjected."

It was only after the door had closed behind him that Mrs. Popescu unfolded the paper that he had given her. As she glanced over it she gave an exclamation that caused her son to look up inquiringly.

"Come here," she said to him, and, when he approached, she put her arms around him. "The Doctor asked this to be taken seriously, and he has ordered—"

Jonitza's eyes grew round with something like terror, as he fixed them on her.

"It's nothing bad. Do look natural," his mother hastily continued. "He has simply ordered me—to take you to spend a month on a farm near some springs in the foot-hills!"

CHAPTER II

JONITZA GETS INTERESTED

Evidently the Doctor did see Jonitza's father, for before the week was ended it had been definitely decided that as soon as the weather was a little warmer Mrs. Popescu would leave with her son for a month's stay in the country. Jonitza had been a trifle interested at first, then he had grumbled, and, finally, he had resumed the languid air that was so peculiarly trying to those about him.

There was one thing in particular that he rebelled against even in his languid state and that was the fact that every afternoon he was now bundled up and ordered out-of-doors for an hour.

"I don't want to go," he would say every time; and every time his mother would kiss him and answer sweetly, "It is for your own good. We must do what the Doctor orders."

Then he would go out into the garden with its lilac and acacia bushes that were just beginning to show leaf buds and walk slowly up and down or stand first on one foot and then on the other as if unable to decide what to do. But one day things went differently. Whether it was due to the air having a genuine spring flavor for the first time that year, or to the fact that it was a holiday and he had been left at home with a couple of servants, or to the fact that the departure for the foot-hills had been definitely set for the first day of the following week, or to some other entirely different cause, in any case there was quite an alert look about the boy and even something of a sparkle in his eyes.

Maritza, the maid, noticed it and remarked to the cook: "Master Jonitza looks quite spry to-day. If he were well, I'd warrant he would get into some mischief." Then she forgot all about him.

A group of boys that Jonitza knew slightly passed by and one seeing him called out: "Come on with us. We're going to the marsh." To his own surprise, Jonitza called back, "All right," and joined them.

When they reached a marshy plain bordering on the Danube some of the boys left them, and Jonitza found himself alone with two boys, both younger than himself. All three were tired from the walk, and finding the stump of an old tree, sat down on it and amused themselves counting the ducks that they saw. Suddenly something that his tutor had told him occurred to Jonitza. "Do you know," he said, "that there are more varieties of ducks on the Danube than in most parts of the world? Let's see how many different ones we can make out."

The little boys did not take kindly to the suggestion. "I am hungry," one of them said; "let's go home."

So back the three began to trudge, now and then throwing a stone into the air, or, when they could, into the water.

Jonitza felt more tired than he cared to confess to the two youngsters and inwardly planned to lie down as soon as he came within doors. "I'll be home in less than fifteen minutes, now!" he suddenly exclaimed, thinking aloud.

"How can you and see me dance?" said a voice behind him so unexpectedly that Jonitza jumped. Turning, he saw a laughing peasant all decorated with tiny bells.

"Oh, jolly!" the other boys shouted. "There's going to be a dance! Come on!"

Those little bells must have said "Come on" too, for Jonitza found himself trying to keep up with the peasant's rapid strides.

Down in the Lower Town, before one of the old domed churches, they found a crowd gathered. Although there was nothing unusual about such a gathering, one could see from the faces that something unusual was expected.

It was not a silent expectation, however. Everywhere people were talking and laughing and a few young men were even singing. As soon as the peasant with bells appeared, a shout arose. At the same instant a troop of other peasants, all attired in their gay embroidered national costumes, with bells at their girdles and on their sleeves, came in a body into the square, and taking their places began to dance and shout and sing and stamp their feet. Some one said this was the Pyrrhic Dance that was sacred in ancient mythology, and that had come to the Roumanians from their Roman forefathers; a dance to prevent Saturn from hearing the voice of his infant son Jupiter, lest he devour him. Whether this explained it or not there was no doubt of the audience liking it, for at its conclusion all clapped their hands and burst into boisterous exclamations of delight. Jonitza, feeling some of the excitement, clapped too, and no longer conscious of any tired feeling waited until almost every one had gone before he made his way slowly home.

CHAPTER III

THE TRIP TO THE COUNTRY

On Tuesday of the following week Jonitza, his mother, and the maid Maritza, after a short trip on the train, were being driven over the vast level and wonderfully fertile plains of Roumania, that stretched before them like a great green sea. There were already signs that the short spring that Roumania has would soon change into summer. Wild flowers were to be seen here and there and birds twittered and flew about.

The way lay among thatched farm-houses whose gleaming walls showed that they had been freshly whitewashed at Easter. Now and then a peasant seated in a rude wagon, drawn by beautiful, creamy, short-legged oxen with wide-spreading horns, saluted them gravely.

At a little elevation in the road they passed a group of dug-outs called bordei, with turf-covered roofs and shapeless clay chimneys. The windows in these bordei were merely irregular holes in the mud walls. At the door leading down into one of these primitive houses stood an attractive looking woman, with a bright yellow kerchief over her head, and another around her neck. She was busily spinning while she crooned a lullaby to a baby who lay blinking its eyes in an oval wooden box swinging from the branches of a tree near by.

Not far from these bordei was a cemetery filled with crosses of the oddest possible shapes. It really seemed as if the people had tried to find a new design for each new grave.

They passed wayside crosses also, before some of which peasants were kneeling in prayer.

But, despite these interesting things, there was something tiring in the long journey over the monotonously level plains, and Jonitza grew more and more restless. His pretty mother noticed it and drawing him to her she began to tell him the most interesting stories. First of all about Trajan, the great Roman Emperor, who came to their country so many centuries ago and conquered the people who then inhabited it. She described to him the great column in Rome commemorating his victory, and told him how proud every Roumanian was that he was descended from the soldiers that the Emperor left to guard the new possessions.

"Is that why we call the thunder Trajan's voice?" asked Jonitza.

"Perhaps," his mother answered. "We certainly love to call things by his name."

"The Milky Way is Trajan's Road, isn't it?" again inquired Jonitza.

His mother nodded.

"The boys call the ditch by the lumber mill Trajan's Moat," Jonitza continued.

His mother smiled. "Roumania is full of Trajan's moats; it would be hard to find a village that hasn't one. There are many interesting stories," continued his mother, "connected with our history. You know, from your tutor, that the section of Roumania in which we live is called Moldavia. Would you like to hear the old legend as to how it got its name?"

"Please tell it to me," her son answered eagerly, his eyes sparkling with interest.

"Once upon a time," began his mother, "a Prince called Bogdan lived in this part of the world. Now, Bogdan had a dog whom he valued above all the other dogs that he owned.

"One day, while out hunting, this dog, whose name was Molda, caught sight of a buffalo and chased it to the very brink of a river. When the terrified buffalo waded into the water the dog in his excitement followed, was caught in the current and drowned.

"When his followers saw how deeply affected by the dog's death Bogdan was, they pursued the buffalo, killed it, and taking its head back with them, nailed it over the entrance to the Palace.

"But this did not lessen the Prince's grief. Whenever possible he would go to the river's banks to mourn. The people, seeing him there, would repeat the story, so that after a while the river became associated with the name of the dog and was spoken of as the Moldava. Gradually the name, slightly modified, was applied also to all of the surrounding country."

"Please tell me more stories about Moldavia," begged Jonitza, when his mother had been silent for some time.

"Listen then to the story of Movila," again began his mother, glad to see that the restless look had left her son's face. "This is a story of King Stephen who was great in mind but very small in body. Once in a battle with Hungarians his horse was killed under him. As the horse fell, the King was caught by one of his heralds, a man as large as Stephen was small. After assisting him to his feet, the herald offered Stephen his own horse. The King looked up at the big animal with a frown, but the herald, kneeling before him, placed Stephen's foot on his shoulder and exclaimed: 'Oh, Prince, allow me to serve you as a mole-hill.'

"'Mole-hill,' returned Stephen, getting on the horse, 'I will make a mountain of you.'

"Then Fortune favored Stephen and soon the victory was his. No sooner was he back in camp than he sent for the herald. When the latter came, he found Stephen surrounded by his court. 'Herald,' said Stephen, 'thou hast served me as a mole-hill. In return I give thee the name of Movila (little mountain). Thou shalt have no other. Thou gavest me thy horse in my need. In return, I give thee five full domains over which thou shalt rule.'"

The carriage here stopped before a tiny tavern in a little vineyard surrounded town. They were disappointed in finding that they could get nothing for lunch except raw onions with salt and mamaliga, the cold corn meal mush that is eaten everywhere throughout peasant Roumania. At first Mrs. Popescu thought they would eat from their own well-filled lunch basket, but when Maritza remarked that mamaliga was really very good, she changed her mind. Then, as they seated themselves before a table on the vine-covered veranda, she asked Maritza to tell them how the mamaliga is prepared.

"The water must be hot," said the maid, "before the meal is stirred into it. You continue stirring until it is almost done, then you can add a little grated cheese. At our house, when it is well cooked, we put it into a cloth and tie it up."

Here some dried fish which the owner of the tavern had perhaps not intended to serve at first, were laid on the table.

"These fish have a nice flavor," remarked Mrs. Popescu.

"I know how they also are prepared," said Maritza, "for my brother has helped get them ready."

"Suppose you tell us about it, Maritza," said Mrs. Popescu, evidently not wishing the party to hurry.

"Very well, ma'am," consented the maid. "First, a kind of basket work of osiers is built up. This is covered with walnut leaves in which the fish are wrapped. The building is then filled with smoke for several days, or until the fish look yellow and smell good. They are then taken down, made into bundles and surrounded by pine-tree branches, which add a new flavor to them that most people like."

Here the tavern-keeper again appeared with a bottle of the damson plum brandy for which Roumania is famous. But Mrs. Popescu shook her head. "Not this time," she said smiling.

From this little town the journey was a steady climb upward amid oak, beech and lime-trees. There were more crosses along the roadside. In one spot there was a large group of them, all brightly painted and roofed over.

It was not until late in the afternoon that they came in sight of the village near which the farm lay where they were to stay for a while. Full of expectations of a good supper, they drove past it and on to a pleasant and prosperous looking dwelling. In the front of the broad veranda an interesting group stood waiting to welcome them.

CHAPTER IV

THE JOURNEY'S END

The medium-sized, vigorous-looking man who formed one of the group on the veranda, hurried forward to meet them. He was dark with long black wavy hair. He wore white woolen trousers, a sort of big sleeved tunic or shirt of coarse but very clean linen, well belted in at the waist by a broad scarlet woolen scarf. Over this was a sleeveless sheepskin jacket, the wool inside, the outside gayly embroidered. On his feet were goatskin sandals.

His wife was slender and quite fair. Like her husband, she was evidently wearing a holiday dress. This was a white gown covered with red and black embroidery, a brightly colored apron, and several necklaces of colored beads and coins. A gay kerchief, fringed with a row of spangles, was set well back on her light brown hair. She also advanced to meet the newcomers.

A bright-eyed boy of about twelve and a very pretty girl about four years younger were left standing and staring by the doorway. After greetings had been exchanged and all had descended from the carriage, the farmer said something to his son who immediately went up to Jonitza and offered him his hand. At the same time he proposed showing him the grounds while supper was being placed on the table.

Jonitza at once accepted the offer. He was anxious to see what was outside, and, besides, his legs felt so stiff from the long ride that he longed to exercise them.

Neither of the boys spoke at first, although they glanced shyly at each other now and then. At a corner of the house the ice was broken in an unexpected fashion. They walked right into a flock of geese who set up a "Honk! Honk!" and made a peck at Jonitza who happened to disturb them most.

Taken by surprise, Jonitza jumped awkwardly to one side. Nicolaia, his companion, could not restrain a laugh. The next minute, evidently fearing that he had hurt his new acquaintance's feelings, he put his hand on his shoulder in a friendly way and suggested a visit to the pigs.

"Katinka," he called to his sister, who was shyly following them, "go get something to take to the pigs."

Katinka turned obediently and ran into the house. She soon reappeared, carefully holding a pan.

The pigs proved worth visiting. They were of the wild boar species with an upright row of funny hard bristles on their backs. They were so full of play, too, that Jonitza was genuinely sorry to hear the call to supper.

"It's just splendid here!" he whispered to his mother as he saw her for an instant alone before entering the big kitchen which served also as dining-room.

Jonitza now noticed that although the farmer and his son had kept their hats on in the house, they were careful to remove them before sitting down to the meal.

This meal was quite an elaborate one. There was fishroe and olives, mutton and cheese, and rye bread about two inches thick and pierced all over with a fork. This was broken, not cut. There was also a kind of mamaliga cooked in milk and called balmosch. This was placed on the table on a big wooden platter, cut with a string, and eaten with layers of cheese.

CHAPTER V

GETTING ACQUAINTED

Jonitza and his mother were out early next morning after a breakfast of bacon and mamaliga.

The farm-house at which they were staying looked attractive in its cleanliness. It had been recently whitewashed and the doors and window frames painted a bright blue. It was built entirely of timber. The roof consisted of thin strips of wood laid closely row upon row. Near the house were some fruit-trees and lilac bushes and a small flower garden in which basil and gilliflowers, so often mentioned in Roumanian folk songs, were conspicuous.

Inside, the big living-room had a comfortable, homey air. The walls were partially covered with hand-woven tapestries. In one corner was a huge Dutch looking stove, while opposite, under an ikon, stood the primitive loom that is still to be seen in all Roumanian farm-houses. Besides the table on which the meals were served, there were some plain three-legged chairs, a large chest, a smaller table on which the basket of Easter eggs still stood, and a sort of couch which served Nicolaia as a bed at night. Its corn husk mattress had a pretty cover with an embroidered ruffle over it in the daytime. The straw pillows then changed their clothes for more fancy ones and were placed evenly against the wall.

Jonitza was anxious to show his mother the sportive pigs and he lost no time in marching her to them. When she had expressed sufficient admiration, they wandered to the well with its long sweep to which a rock was attached, and crossed themselves before the brightly painted crosses that were on each side of it. Katinka came out with a pitcher while they stood there, and knelt in prayer before the crosses before drawing up the water.

"Where is Nicolaia?" they asked her. She pointed to the cow-shed where they found him hard at work.

He smiled at them in greeting.

"This is my job," he said, "until I take the sheep to pasture in the mountains, for my mother is to let me do so this year."

Jonitza watched his robust companion with some envy as he went cheerfully about what he had to do. Nicolaia did it all easily and quickly; at the same time he did not neglect to make an occasional pleasant remark, and he did this with the courtesy that seems natural to the Roumanian peasant. Among other things he told them the names of some of the beautiful cream-colored oxen that his father owned. They were very high-sounding ones. There were Antony and Cæsar, Cassius and Brutus, Augustus, and, of course, Trajan, the finest-looking creature of all.

Then, almost without warning, the weather changed, a heavy rain setting in. This caused all, except the father who was absent, to gather in the big living-room. Here Katinka, in a matter-of-fact way, took out some embroidery on linen, which at the age of eight she was already getting ready for her bridal trousseau. Later she showed Mrs. Popescu a rug that she was beginning to weave as a covering for her bed.

In the meantime, Mrs. Popescu and Maritza also took out some embroidery, the peasant mother sat down at the loom, and Nicolaia brought out a bit of wood-carving. This, he said, was now being taught in the village school. Jonitza alone had no work. He stood for a while by the window watching the rain splash against it and the wind shake the trees as if it meant to uproot them. It was not long, however, before he wandered to where Nicolaia sat and watched him work.

Mrs. Popescu looked over at her idle son several times. A sudden inspiration made her say: "You seem to carve very nicely, Nicolaia. How would you like to be Jonitza's teacher and earn a little money of your own?"

"Will you?" asked Jonitza dropping on the floor beside Nicolaia. The peasant boy looked up with a pleased smile. "If you think I know enough," he answered modestly, "I'll be glad to teach you."

Here his mother could not keep from remarking with a proud air: "The school teacher takes an interest in Nicolaia. He has advised him to attend the Government School of Fruit Culture which is in the next village from ours. He says he would learn other things besides taking care of fruit-trees there. But that isn't possible, for he's promised as an apprentice to his uncle in Bukurest. Well, he'll learn a great deal there, too."

"Oh, mother," exclaimed Nicolaia when his mother had left the loom and taken up some knitting, "while we are working won't you sing some songs as you do when we're alone?"

His mother's fair face flushed as she looked shyly at Mrs. Popescu. "I must get things ready for the mid-day meal," she said rising.

As soon as her back was turned, Mrs. Popescu nodded to good-natured Maritza who understood and began to sing a song about a heiduk, the traditional hero of the Roumanian peasantry, a person as fascinating as our own Robin Hood. The song told how handsome he was, how winning his ways, how fearless his manner towards tyrants, how kind to the poor and unfortunate.

Nicolaia's mother was back in her place before the maid finished. "That was very nice, dear," she remarked. "And now I can't do less than sing a song, too. It'll be about a woman, the bravest shepherdess that ever was seen."

This was evidently a favorite with the children, for they joined in an odd refrain that occurred every once in a while.

She had scarcely finished when the sun came out to announce that the rain was over. A moment after the door opened and her husband entered.

CHAPTER VI

AN EXCURSION

During the meal that followed, the farmer turned to his son with: "You will have to go to the Convent for me this afternoon. I can't spare the time myself. And perhaps"—here he turned to Mrs. Popescu—"you and your son might like the trip. It would give you a chance to see one of our old-time institutions."

Mrs. Popescu thanked him. "Nothing could be pleasanter," she said.

Soon all three were seated on a rough timber cart with apparently nothing to hold it together. To the cart were harnessed two moody looking buffaloes with horns lying almost flat along their necks. The cart swayed and twisted up the rough road when suddenly Nicolaia gave an excited exclamation. They were just in the middle of one of the great swollen streams that flowed everywhere over the mountains.

"What has happened?" asked Mrs. Popescu anxiously, for Nicolaia was standing up and urging the animals forward.

Nicolaia gave a short, funny laugh. "The buffaloes want to take a bath," he answered, and again shouted at them. Fortunately, after a display of much stubbornness on their part, he did persuade them that neither the time nor the place was suitable for bathing, and they moved slowly on.

After safely passing through all the ruts and bogs, the creaking cart at length stopped before what was called the "Guest House" on one side of an old half-deserted convent. A servant dressed in the national costume, with a wide hat on his long curling hair, came to meet them and bid them welcome. Later one of the inmates, an elderly woman in a loose brown dress, appeared bringing coffee, preserved fruit, and buffalo milk, which Jonitza thought had a very peculiar flavor.

After they had partaken of this refreshment and expressed their appreciation of the courtesy, and while Nicolaia was busy with his errand, Mrs. Popescu and Jonitza visited the church of the Convent and looked at the crude frescoes of heaven and hell that adorned its walls. There were many ikons or pictures of saints about, for Roumania is a Greek Catholic country like Russia. The large size of the Convent showed that it must have enjoyed great prosperity in former times. Now a deep quiet reigned everywhere.

Nicolaia grew quite talkative on the way back; he told of the source of one of the streams that they passed and how difficult it was to get to it, of a hermit cave in another part of the mountains in which the bats fly at you when you enter, and finally, of some of his own immediate plans. He talked at length about a friend called Demetrius, who lived on the other side of the village and whom he planned to see on the following day, when his own work was done. "Would you like to visit him with me?" he asked, turning politely to Jonitza.

"Like!" repeated Jonitza almost rudely. "Of course."

They were passing through the village at the time and Mrs. Popescu noticed that on certain houses a flower was painted. She pointed this out. "That," explained Nicolaia, "is to let every one know that a maiden lives there."

A little further on they met a branch entwined cart. In it sat two girls gayly talking. One of them called to Nicolaia in passing.

The girls did not look at all alike and Mrs. Popescu wondered if they were sisters.

"No," said Nicolaia, "they are only surata, that is, they have adopted each other as sisters. Any girls can do that if they love each other enough. I was at the Church when the ceremony was performed, and saw their feet chained together in token of the bond. It made them the same as born sisters. Sometimes a young man adopts another young man for his brother in the same way. The priest always asks them if they are sure of their affection, for he says the ceremony makes the new relationship very binding."

CHAPTER VII

ST. GEORGE'S DAY

The next day the boys walked over to the home of Nicolaia's village friend, Demetrius, and here a delightful surprise awaited them. Two young bear cubs trotted like dogs at the feet of the village boy as he came to meet them.

"Where did you get these?" both boys shouted with delight.

"From my uncle," returned Demetrius. "He captured them after their mother had been killed. At first they had to be fed sheep milk with a spoon."

As he spoke, one of the little fellows ran up a tree in the yard and the other began to play with a young puppy. Soon the boys were trying to help Demetrius teach them to turn somersaults and do other tricks. They gave this up only when they remembered there were other things to settle before parting. These things all related to St. George's Day, or, as it is sometimes called, the "Witch's Sabbath." This would come the very last of the week. There were mysteries in regard to the day, for the boys spoke in whispers while Jonitza was trying to make one of the bears jump through a hoop. He was so much interested in the antics of the little creatures that he paid no attention until just at leaving he heard something which made him open his eyes wide. Hidden treasure was to be found!

On the way home he answered Nicolaia in monosyllables and looked moody, much to the latter's surprise. "What's the matter?" Nicolaia finally asked.

For answer Jonitza glared and then burst out with: "What have I done that you won't let me go with you on St. George's Eve?"

Nicolaia was taken aback. "You've done nothing," he made haste to say. "But this must be kept a secret and your mother wouldn't like your going."

"I won't tell her," said Jonitza, wincing a little as he spoke; "that is—not until—eh—I show her the treasure. Then she won't care."

Nicolaia looked up and down the road as if trying to find a way out of a difficulty. At last he said faintly, "Well, all right, if you can meet us in the yard by the cow-sheds at ten o'clock."

On the day before the "Witch's Sabbath," Jonitza watched Nicolaia's father cut square blocks of turf and place them before every door and window of the farm-house and stables. "Why are you doing that?" he asked. The farmer smiled at him but did not answer. Katinka, however, came and whispered that it was to keep out the witches. She turned from him to help her father place thorn branches here and there in the cut turf. Jonitza followed every act with a fascinated air. "What's that for?" he asked her. "The witches run when they see thorns," she explained, smiling at the thought.

Two of the men who were helping on the farm at the time, offered to keep watch all night near the stables lest the witches should charm the cattle and do them harm. Mrs. Popescu, who heard them make the offer, asked them if they really believed in witches.

They looked at her with the air of grown up children. "If it wasn't witches," said one with a triumphant air, "what made old Theodoresco's cow give bloody milk last year for several months beginning the very next day after the 'Witch's Sabbath'?" Mrs. Popescu, seeing that it would be useless to argue the question, left them.

A half hour later, Nicolaia appeared and beckoned to Jonitza to follow him indoors. Here he took an earthen jar from a closet. "What do you think that is?" he asked.

"One of your mother's jars," Jonitza answered.

"No," said Nicolaia without smiling. "Put your hand inside and see what you find."

Jonitza did so and brought out some ancient coins dating back to pre-Roman times.

"My father is keeping these for luck. He found them when he was plowing," said Nicolaia. "I am showing this to you because I thought you ought to know that it may be that kind of treasure that we'll find to-night."

Jonitza had this constantly in mind the rest of the day. "How wonderful it would be to find a real treasure," he kept thinking. He ate little for supper, went to bed at once when his mother suggested it, and tried very hard to keep from falling asleep. But alas, despite his efforts, sleep came and it was a very deep sleep, so that when he awoke it was bright morning.

He hurried out, ashamed of himself, and found his friend looking very drowsy and grinning in a somewhat downcast way. In answer to Jonitza's hurried explanations of what had happened to himself and urgent questions, Nicolaia said: "It was just after ten o'clock when we started. I was relieved that you didn't appear, for I didn't know what might happen. There was no moon at the time, but the stars were out, and as we know the hills well, Demetrius and I had no trouble making our way over them. We heard all sorts of strange noises, but we weren't a bit afraid. I thought we should surely find the treasure. You see, they say around here that it is easiest for the one born on a Sunday or at midday; and Demetrius was born just two minutes after noon on a Sunday. So that ought to count.

"We spoke only in whispers as we tried to look in every direction at once. Each of us wanted to be the first to see the blue flame which shows where the treasure lies hidden. It must have been past midnight when Demetrius seized hold of my arm. I felt his hand tremble.

'WE STOOD AS IF PARALYZED'"

"'Do you see that?' he whispered.

"I looked where he pointed and saw in the distance what really seemed like a tiny fire. It was not particularly blue but we did not think of that. I felt for my knife, for it must be thrown through the flame so that the spirits who guard the treasure won't harm you.

"'Have you your knife?' I whispered back.

"'Yes,' returned Demetrius. 'I'll throw first, and if I miss, you throw right after.' Before this we had not minded anything, but now as we crept on, we shuddered whenever we stepped on a dry twig or caused a stone to roll down hill.

"As we came nearer there was no sign of flame but there were bright patches on theground as if from the remains of a fire. This could just be seen around a big bowlder where we stopped for a moment to gain courage for the final step.

"As we stood there we heard a sound as of some creature rolling over. Then on the other side of the big rock, a huge form arose. We distinctly heard some cuss words and a threat so terrible that we stood as if paralyzed. Suddenly the figure began to move, and forgetful of everything else but our own safety, we ran down the hillside, stumbling over each other, now rolling a way, tearing our clothes on thorn bushes, and generally having a hard time until we both landed in a brook. We crawled out very much chilled and stood listening. Everything about us was quiet, so I don't know whether we were followed or not. However, we did not dare return.

"So, of course, we didn't get any treasure. My father says it was probably some old gypsy, but I know it was a bad spirit, for as I have said, it was after midnight, and good spirits show the flame only till twelve. When it is seen later, the treasure is guarded by bad spirits."

CHAPTER VIII

THE CASTLE OF STEPHEN THE GREAT

How quickly the month at the farm-house passed! Every day there was so much to see and do, and once in a while there was an excursion to some place of interest. The furthest one taken was when Jonitza and Katinka went with the maid who had accompanied Jonitza's mother to the country, for a couple of days' visit to her home in a place called Niamtz.

The day after they reached the straggling village, the children were allowed out to play. They were attracted to a great red earth cliff, where they began digging tunnels and building little cave houses. Tiring of that they wandered up toward the cliff's summit, gathering the beautiful wild flowers that they found on the way, and resting now and then under some leafy tree. When they reached the top they both shouted with delight at finding the ruins of a castle. What a delightful place in which to play! There were four corner towers, strong buttresses and battlemented walls, as well as a large moat all the way around, now overgrown with trees.

Jonitza, who was blessed with a good memory, recalled what he had been told about the place and so hastened to instruct Katinka in his own fashion, emphasizing every word that he considered of importance. "This," said he, in his tutor's manner, "is the old castle celebrated in many of our songs, of one of our greatest kings called Stephen the Great.

"One day, Stephen the Great was fighting the Turks who were winning. He thought it was no use fighting any longer and made for home as quickly as he could. He thought his mother would be glad he wasn't killed. But instead of that she met him at the big gate you see over there, and told him he ought to be ashamed to give up; that he was fighting to free his people, and that she wouldn't ever open the gates to him and his army unless he came back as victor." (Here Jonitza gave an especial emphasis to the last word.) "So Stephen said, 'All right,' and went back. He met the Turks in a narrow valley and was so mad that he killed almost every one of them. He was a very brave man, and I'm going to be like him."

These last words were hardly spoken when there was a clap of thunder and flash of lightning, followed by a sudden heavy downpour of rain. The children hurried to shelter which they found in one of the towers.

"IT WAS ONLY MARITZA"

It was dark there and the wind and rain threatened to break through the walls. Bat-like things flew about, and strange noises, like the mournful voices of imprisoned spirits, began to be heard. Jonitza lost his brave air entirely as he and his companion crouched side by side against one of the walls. Suddenly there was a peculiarly long whistle, probably made by the wind passing through some crevice. Katinka gave a little shriek. "It is the Stafii," she cried, clinging to her friend.

Jonitza, though trembling, put his arm around her. He knew very well that she was referring to harmful elves whom all the Roumanian country folk believe dwell in ruins and are always unfriendly to human beings. He tried to think of something comforting to say, but at first only managed to clear his throat. After a bit what he did whisper was: "We ought to have some milk to give them." At this Katinka cried more than ever. "That's what they say, but we haven't any, we haven't any," she repeated almost in a shriek.

This was followed by another shriek as a dark form shut out what little light reached them. But it was only Maritza, who had come with a big umbrella to their rescue.

CHAPTER IX

A SPINNING BEE

The evening before they left Niamtz, a crowd of Maritza's girl friends gathered at her home for a Spinning Bee.

They came with heads uncovered, for only married women in Roumania wear veils or kerchiefs. They were all dressed in holiday finery, with their hair beautifully waved.

At first a merry little maiden with very red cheeks, and very black eyebrows over sparkling eyes, and black hair twisted into a double plait, came in for a good deal of teasing for some reason or other. She didn't seem to mind it and her bright answers caused much laughter and good feeling. Finally she succeeded in drawing attention from herself by asking a riddle. This was followed by another and another until everybody in the room was guessing.

Then Maritza's mother, who had been busy getting refreshments ready, came in exclaiming, "Time for work, girls!"

At this there was a general cry of "Maritza!" "We want Maritza!" "Maritza must be our leader!"

Maritza stepped forward with some show of reluctance. "There are better spinners and better singers than I am," she said modestly. But the girls, rising quickly, formed a ring around her, singing in chorus, "It's you we want."

Then Maritza took her spindle and began to spin. At the same time she improvised a strange song all about a mysterious heiduk or chieftain who passed through their village. Suddenly she threw her spindle to the black-eyed, red-cheeked maiden, holding it by a long thread as she did so. The merry maiden caught it and was obliged to continue both the spinning and singing while Maritza pulled out the flax. This required much dexterity.

When each girl had had her turn, both in spinning and singing, refreshments were passed around. There was mamaliga, baked pumpkin, potatoes, and last of all, plenty of popcorn.

Then, while all seated resumed their work, one of their number was begged for a story.

She smilingly consented, and told the following strange and pathetic tale.

THE STORY OF A LILAC TREE

"This is a story of what once must have taken place, for if it had never occurred, I would not now have it to tell.

"In a little valley among the high mountains, there lived a maiden all alone. She worked all day at her spinning and weaving and sang with joy as she worked.

"So the years went on, each year adding loveliness to her face and figure. One day when out gathering firewood for her small needs she heard what sounded like a cry of pain. Making her way into the thicket she found a man sorely wounded.

"She spoke to him but he had become unconscious, and, not knowing what else to do, she took him in her strong arms and carried him to her hut and laid him on her own bed. Then she washed out his wounds and tended him like a sister.

"As soon as he could speak, he tried to express his gratitude. 'Dear maiden,' he said, 'had it not been for you I should never again have seen the light of day, and even as it is, I fear I shall never walk again. For it was no ordinary mortal by whom I was wounded, but a demon of some kind who threatened that even should I survive, all power to move my legs will have left me. Of what good will life then be to me? Trouble yourself no longer, sweet maiden, to cure me. Rather let my wounds bleed anew.'

"But the beautiful girl shook her head. 'Why should we believe all that ill?' she said. 'I am skilled in herb lore and shall cure you.'

"For more than a week the man lay in bed while the girl tended him. And she grew to love him, he was so patient, so grateful for all she did. Then, one morning, he looked brightly at her: 'Lo, I am cured.' And he sat up in bed. But when he tried to get down he could not.

"And the next day it was the same and the next. But the man did not speak of any disappointment. Instead, he told his nurse strange stories of the life he had seen, and one day something that she found hard to bear. It was of the beautiful woman whom he loved and would have wed.

"The maiden, though now sad, still tended him faithfully, but to no avail. At last, in her distress, she sought out a witch who was famed for her wisdom over the whole mountain side.

"'The man is under enchantment,' said the old woman. 'He knows his cure, but will not tell it to thee.'

"'Tell me what it is!' exclaimed the maiden. 'I will pay any price for the cure!'

"'Are you sure?' asked the witch with a disagreeable laugh.

"'I am sure,' answered the maiden.

"'Know then,' said the witch, 'that only a virgin life like yours can save him. Will you give your life?'

"The girl looked down in thought. At last she spoke. 'If it is indeed so, why should I not? He is strong again and the world has need of him. He loves another from whom only bewitchment separates him. The happiness of two is worth the sacrifice of one. I will give my life that they may wed.'

"The next morning when the man made his daily trial to arise, he found to his amazement that he could do so. He looked around for the maiden, but she was nowhere to be seen. He waited all day and till the next morning but she did not come. Then, full of regret, he went away. Near the threshold of the hut he stopped to pick a branch of fragrant lilac. As he did so, the whole bush swayed with delight, and it seemed to him that a spirit within it called his name as he turned away."

CHAPTER X

NEW PLANS

Jonitza tried to forget that the time for leaving the country was approaching. The month had meant much to him. It had made a remarkable change in his appearance. His listless air had given way to a wide awake interested look, and his pale cheeks had already something of a ruddy hue.

Although for her own sake, Mrs. Popescu longed for a return home, she felt something like guilt in taking her son back with her. Every night she gave much thought to the subject and every night she knelt in prayer before the ikon that hung in her bedroom, asking that light be given her as to her duty. Finally, unable to decide, she wrote a long letter to her busy husband and begged his advice.

Instead of a written answer, her husband himself arrived. His solution of the difficulty startled her.

"Why shouldn't Jonitza accompany Nicolaia as a sheep herder into the Carpathians?"

"I'm afraid," she said, "there are gypsies there—and bad shepherds—and wild animals—and the life is too hard."

Her husband made light of all these things. "I've talked it over," he said, "with the Doctor. He declares that the only trouble with our boy is that we've molly-coddled him. He advised me to trust him to Nicolaia, whose family he knows. He says that Jonitza is just the age to enjoy the experience and that he will thank us all his life for it."

But at first Mrs. Popescu did not agree. "He has grown much heartier," she said. "Perhaps he would get along very well at home now."

So it was not settled until after the whole thing was talked over with the peasant and his wife and Mrs. Popescu was persuaded that her son would be in safe hands and that, besides, the dangers were less than in the city. Then Katinka was sent to call in the boys who were busy as usual with some outside work. They came in with a surprised air, but when all was explained to them both set up a shout that echoed from the darkened rafters of the room.

Mr. Popescu laughed with pleasure. "Can that be really my son?" he said.

CHAPTER XI

IN THE CARPATHIANS

"I feel as free as a bird!" Jonitza could not help exclaiming when they had actually started with their flocks for the Carpathian mountains. Like his friend, he was dressed in typical shepherd costume, consisting of a coarse white linen shirt and trousers, a long mantle of very heavy wool, and a straight round sheepskin cap. His very shoes were the same, for the boys had fashioned both pair together. They were made of pieces of goatskin that had been soaked in water until soft, gathered into pleats by means of thongs over the ankles, while other bits of thong held them securely in place.

They had a big flock of sheep under their charge, for besides those belonging to Nicolaia's father they were to herd those belonging to the richest man in that neighborhood. Besides the sheep, two intelligent wolf dogs belonging to the neighbor went with them, as well as a donkey, to be used later to carry the packs of cheese and milk.

It was high time for the boys to start, for the other shepherds had gone, and the hot Roumanian summer was beginning to be felt.

Although Nicolaia had already spent two summers on the mountains this was the first time that he was in charge of so large a flock. In consequence he shared some of Jonitza's excitement. There was another reason why this summer might prove a notable one for him. It was probably his last experience of the kind, for his parents had decided to have him apprenticed that autumn to his uncle, a cabinet maker in the city of Bukurest, and apprenticeships in Roumania are for six years.

It was a hard climb for the boys. At first as they made their way upward they occasionally passed one-room shanties, each shared by an entire family and all the domestic animals. At the last one of these they stopped to ask for a drink of water. The door was open and inside they could see the scanty furniture—a rude table, a bench, a stove, and a cot covered with the skins of wild beasts. A fierce looking man answered their call and handed them the water with so surly an air that Nicolaia, who was accustomed to the great hospitality of the section where he lived, felt a mingling of amazement and indignation. There was no garden of any kind around this house, but there was a wealth of wild flowers. Yellow foxgloves, gladiolas, and wild honeysuckle seemed determined to make the place a thing of beauty.

Just at noon, near one of the little streams that constantly crossed their path, they came upon a small band of the gypsies that are as numerous in Roumania as in Hungary. By a small fire over which a kettle hung, sat two women. A short distance from them lay a dark-skinned lad, with matted hair, while leaning against a giant beech on the other side, was a young man playing a weird air that made one think of a mountain storm, on a crude violin.

From this wayside camp, the path wound around and around until at last it suddenly branched into two parts. Nicolaia stopped at this point perplexed. "I do not remember this," he said, as he chose the broader looking of the two roads. Soon, however, he saw the mistake he made in doing so. What he had taken for a path was the channel of a mountain torrent. It ended in a steep abyss, down which some of the sheep had already scrambled.

The boys spent fully half an hour of the hardest kind of work before they got these sheep back. When, shortly after, they came to a grassy valley, both, panting hard, threw themselves under a tree.

"This is where we'll camp for the night," said Nicolaia, "now that we have all the sheep together." As he spoke, he unpacked the supper of cold meat, onions, and mamaliga that they had brought with them. They also helped themselves to a drink of sheep's milk, which is richer and thicker than cow's and of quite a different flavor.

The sun was already low, and when it sank from sight, darkness followed very soon. Quickly wrapping themselves in their mantles, the boys lay down beside their sheep. So strenuous had the day been, that hardly had they exchanged a few sentences than both were fast asleep.

The next day, after an early breakfast, they were again on their way. The scenery around was grandly wild. Enormous birch and oak-trees towered on both sides of the narrow path, while lime-trees gave forth the honeyed sweetness of their blossoms. Here and there a precipice would yawn on one side of the pathway. No homes of any kind were to be seen.

The afternoon was far advanced when they reached another valley which was to form their headquarters for the summer. Several of the shepherds who shared this section noted their arrival and sent a welcome to them on their boutchoums, long pipes of cherry wood which can be heard for a great distance. In the Middle Ages, Roumanians used the boutchoums to proclaim war to the troops.

Nicolaia at once led Jonitza to a sort of cave formed of large, loose stones. "This," he said, "is the store-house of six or eight of us who herd in this vicinity."

The next morning the work began in earnest. Some of it was splendid training. Each day Nicolaia and Jonitza had to creep along the crags with the flocks. Sometimes the footing was very insecure, so it was no wonder that at the end of the first day Jonitza was covered with bruises from his many falls. "I'm as stiff as a board, too," he confided to Nicolaia, as they lay down near each other to sleep. But, by the end of the week, the stiffness was entirely gone, and Jonitza could manage to keep his footing on the rocks even better than Nicolaia. By that time, too, he had learned the call that would make the sheep clinging to the steep mountainsides stop eating, look up, and then come scrambling to him.

The donkey had been let loose as soon as the valley was reached and got into all kinds of scrapes from his dislike to being alone. Sometimes when he found that he couldn't follow the sheep, he would stand on a bowlder and bray loudly as if proclaiming to an unsympathetic world his loneliness.

Sometimes the report would spread that wild animals had been seen prowling near. This meant extra watchfulness on the part of the shepherds. But whether there was reason for any especial alarm or not, every night each shepherd wrapped himself in his sheepskin or woolen mantle and lay down by his flock ready to spring up at the least sign of danger.

CHAPTER XII

IN THE CARPATHIANS (Continued)

Although Jonitza and Nicolaia could not be constantly together, they tried to share at least one meal every day. Once at such a time Jonitza remarked: "How I wish I could get to the top of that mountain yonder. See what a queer shape it is! It makes me think of the picture of a peak called 'La Omu,' the man."

Nicolaia thought that a funny name. "How did it come to get it?" he asked.

"Let me think," replied Jonitza. "Oh, yes, I remember now what was written about it in my story book. It said that it had another name, 'Negoi,' but that most of the country people preferred 'La Omu' because of its resemblance to a human figure. When one came near he could see that this was caused by a big rock in the center of a mass of others. According to tradition, a shepherd once lost his way there and began to curse God for his misfortune. Suddenly as he was cursing, God turned him into stone as a warning to others."

"Although that probably isn't 'La Omu,'" said Nicolaia, "I should like to climb it nevertheless. Perhaps Vasili would keep an eye on our sheep for a few hours if we asked him."

"Do you think so?" asked Jonitza eagerly. And he at once ran to a bluff and shouted to Vasili, who was stationed nearer to them than any of the other shepherds. Vasili called back good-naturedly, "Go on. I'll see the sheep don't wander far." And the boys started.

It took them half an hour to reach the peak. Gradually, as they ascended it, the pine and fir-trees dwindled into misshapen goblin-like bushes, each of which seemed to be hiding behind one of the great bowlders that were everywhere so plentiful.

"THERE . . . LAY TWO LONG SHINY SNAKES"

At one point the boys were clambering up a steep rocky path when suddenly Jonitza gave a shriek and at the same time jumped high into the air. Nicolaia, who was a short distance behind, stopped so suddenly that he almost lost his balance. There, stretched out between the two boys, lay two long shiny snakes sunning themselves and apparently paying no heed to what had happened.

Nicolaia recovered himself first. He grasped tight hold of his shepherd staff and approached. "Pshaw!" he called disdainfully, to Jonitza on the other side. "They're harmless." Then jumping without fear over them, he ran to where his companion, panting hard, was leaning against a bowlder.

Seeing an open space near, the boys looked it over carefully and sat down. "It was the suddenness of seeing the snakes that made me jump," said Jonitza, apparently feeling that his natural action needed explanation. At this Nicolaia chuckled and then began to lecture Jonitza on the necessity of always keeping wide awake in the mountains and never allowing himself to be surprised.

Jonitza did not relish this and interrupted his companion to ask questions. "How is one to tell harmless snakes from others? Have you ever seen snakes just born?"

At this last question, Nicolaia's eyes flashed. "How I wish I could find a snake's nest!" he exclaimed. "Don't you know that precious stones are made from snake saliva? If I found a snake nest, I'd not run but kill the snakes, and then I'd be so rich I'd be able to buy a big farm of my own."

An answering flash came into Jonitza's eyes. "Let's go hunt for one now," he said, springing up. Nicolaia rose more slowly. "I'm willing, but I warn you that we must be careful."

So with their long shepherd staves in their hands, and keeping watch where they trod, they began a hunt among the bowlders.

How it might have ended no one can tell, for they had gone scarcely twenty yards when they heard a loud cry from down below.

"It must be for us," said Nicolaia, and quite forgetful of snakes or anything else he led the way back as fast as he was able.

When they reached the slopes on which their sheep were grazing, they met a shout of laughter. "It was your donkey," Vasili explained. "He tried, as usual, to follow the flock and this time slipped down between two rocks and couldn't go forward or back. Didn't you hear him bray? I didn't know what to do and so called for you. But in the meantime this other Vasili here came bounding up from nowhere. And you ought to have seen him manage! He tied the donkey's feet together with a thong and lifted him out as easily as one would a baby."

"You know you helped me," said a new voice.

The boys looked up to see a stranger standing near. He was of medium height but thickset and very hardy in appearance. Instead of a sheepskin cap a broad-brimmed hat was set well back over a mass of glossy black curls. His features were regular; his eyes were now smiling but there were angry lines written long before around them. The boys shook hands with him and thanked him. "It was nothing," he said. "Aren't we brothers?"

"Where are you from?"

"I belong to the other side," the youth answered, and then added, "The side that isn't free."

All knew at once that he referred to Transylvania, which, although a part of Hungary, is largely inhabited by Roumanians.

"We intend to make it free," Nicolaia answered with feeling. The Transylvanian smiled and shook his head. Then, without a word more, he left them.

There was one other shepherd that they learned to know. He was the oldest there and came from Jassy, once the capital of Moldavia, a city so old that the Turks claim that it dates back to the time of Abraham. The Roumanians, however, feel that they can do better than that. They put its foundations to the time of their beloved Trajan!

This shepherd, of whom later they heard strange wild tales, kept much to himself. Often, however, the monotonously melancholy notes of a wooden flute on which he played would reach them. Sometimes, too, especially at early dawn, they would hear him draw forth powerful notes on theboutchoum, such as no other shepherd could equal.

CHAPTER XIII

LEAVING THE MOUNTAINS

Thus the summer slowly passed in healthy out-of-door life that began to grow exceedingly monotonous at the end. It was lonely, too, for after the boys became used to the work even the noon meals together became rarer, and sometimes several days passed with no other communication than a few calls to each other.

At last September came. This is the month when the herdsmen take their sheep again to the valleys. The donkey was laden with cheeses of sheep's milk, and the boys followed the procession back to the village from which they had started. They found it delightful to be together again, and somehow, as they talked it over, the summer experience that had begun to be trying regained its charm.

They joked, they told folk tales, and Nicolaia even sang a ballad that had long been a favorite with the Roumanians. It was very touching, and, of course, had to do with a shepherd, of his love for his sheep and his dogs and his longing to lie near them even in death.

Long before they reached the farm-house they had been seen by Katinka who ran out to meet them.

Jonitza found some letters awaiting him. He picked out the daintiest, knowing it to be from his mother, and, begging to be excused, tore it open to read immediately.

It was from Sinaia, the fashionable mountain resort where "Carmen Sylva," the late loved dowager Queen Elizabeth, had had her summer home.

"Your father," said the letter among other things, "has to make a business trip among our Wallachian farmers. He intends to take you with him and finally spend a day or two with me here. Later on, we shall visit relatives for some time at the capital, Bukurest."

Two days later Mr. Popescu took his son away.

As Mr. Popescu's business was with the peasants, most of the trip was made by carriage through the very rich agricultural sections of Wallachia.

Now they stopped at the farms of the wealthy, where the very latest in farm machinery could be seen at work; then at some of the hundreds of small farms where the peasants still harvested their grain with the sickle, and threshed it with the flail. On the way they passed orchards of damson plum, from which brandy is made, and vineyards with their rich yield.

The weather favored them. Only once were they caught in a storm. The sky directly above had been monotonously blue for several days when clouds seemed suddenly to form in all directions. A wind arose that soon changed into a tempest, raising enormous clouds of dust. Angry lightning began to fly across the sky, while not only the thunder but the storm itself threatened. Through the dust they could just make out a tower which showed that they were near a village. The obedient horses strained every sinew to reach it and did just manage to get under cover at a rude inn when enormous hail stones began to fall.

It proved to be rather an interesting place where they had secured shelter, for it was not only an inn but a general store where a little of everything was kept for sale. As no especial room was assigned them, Jonitza felt free to wander about the place. On a sort of screened back porch he found a woman pickling whole heads of cabbage, adding corn-meal to the brine to hasten fermentation. This, when stuffed with chopped pork, onions and rice, forms one of the national dishes.

Mr. Popescu smiled at the supper that was placed before them an hour later. There was, of course, mamaliga and its string, with a big pitcher of rich milk, then some salted cheese, raw onions, and some sun-dried beef that had been seasoned with spices and garlic when cooked. The platters, spoons and forks were of wood, the knives alone being of steel.

Although the owner of the inn was evidently pleased at having so much to place before his guests, he seemed to think that he could do still better. "One of my pigs," he said, "is to be killed to-morrow. If you will stay till then I can offer you something really fine."

Although that might not have been the reason, Mr. Popescu decided to stay.

"Come," the landlord's wife said to Jonitza next morning as he sat on the stoop in front of the inn. In answer to her mysterious beckoning, Jonitza followed her to the rear. Here he found a group of men and boys gathered around a big fire from which a very pleasant odor rose.

"What is it?" Jonitza inquired. The landlady laughed and then whispered, "The pig has been killed and we are burning off its hair."

After the meat had been exposed to the heat for a sufficient length of time, thin slices were cut off and handed to each person present. This resulted in loud exclamations from some of the children whose fingers were burnt and even louder smacking of lips as the delicious morsels were tasted.

They left late that afternoon for the next village, overtaking on the way a party of reapers with scythes over their shoulders. A young woman crowned with wheaten ears led several others, all of whom chanted some melancholy air about the end of the harvest.

Everywhere they went people sang, the number of folk songs about soldier life being particularly noticeable. Many of these songs were exceedingly touching; some, however, were wild in character. All were full of a spirit of rare bravery and resignation to whatever fate had in store.

At last among the grand forests near the Prahova River, the pretty rustic houses of rural Roumania changed to Swiss looking cottages, and then to fine brown and red-roofed villas, hotels and baths. Sinaia had been reached.

A little apart from the villas stood the Royal Summer Palace, with its tall roofs and glittering pinnacles.

During the trip they had changed vehicles and drivers many times, and now a very old man acted as their coachman. His eyes sparkled as he pointed out the Château. "I lived near here," he said, "when this Château was built for King Carol and Queen Elizabeth, whom they tell me is now generally called 'Carmen Sylva.' My daughter was better acquainted with her than I. Might I tell you the story, sir? It was not long after the Château was finished that the King and Queen drove up to spend a few days here. They had splendid horses and came fast. My little girl was playing by the roadside and somehow frightened the horses for they leaped to one side. They were brought under control at once, but the child had been more frightened than they and cried loudly.

"Her Majesty must have heard her for she ordered the coachman to stop. When he had done so, she herself got out and went back to my little one, whom she comforted in a few minutes. As she kissed her and put some coins in her hands, she whispered, 'Be ready to pay me a visit to-morrow morning. I'll come for you.'

"We did not think anything of this, but the next day, sure enough, a carriage came to our little hut for Florica. You can imagine our excitement until we had our little one again and heard from her the whole story of her visit to Fairy Land, for that is what the visit to the Château was to her.

"But I have another and better reason to bless her Gracious Majesty. My brother, sir, was blind — couldn't see a thing, sir — and our Queen made him happy, as she did others like him, in the Asylum for the Blind that she founded in Bukurest.

"She was always doing good.

"She liked our peasant ways, sir, she did, and our dress. In the Château she always wore the national costume and all her maids had to do so. Deeper in the woods is a Forester's hut where they tell me she wrote stories and songs like our own."

As the man chatted they approached a deep-roofed chalet from which the sound of merry laughter and conversation was wafted down to them. Then they stopped before it and the next moment Jonitza was in his mother's arms.

CHAPTER XIV

THE CAPITAL OF ROUMANIA

Jonitza had not been a week in Bukurest when he began to wish himself back in the country. At first there had been much to see, especially in the fine shops on the beautiful street called Calea Vittoriei, which extends from one end of the city to the other. On this street is also the Royal Palace and most of the theaters.

Jonitza and his parents were staying with near relatives in one of the many fine residential sections, where the big stone houses are surrounded by beautiful gardens.

Although this section was no great distance from the business center, they never walked to the latter but either drove or went in the big touring car belonging to the family.

"People must be very happy in the 'City of Pleasure,'"—that is what the word Bukurest means—Jonitza said to himself one day as he watched the very lively crowds on the streets. He was standing at the time in front of the splendid show windows of a jewelry store, waiting for his mother who had gone inside. At first he had stared at the rich gems through the glass but the interesting passing crowd had gradually attracted him; the very fashionable ladies, some light, some dark, talking so vivaciously, the priests with their long hair, and, most of all, the numerous soldiers in the splendor and variety of their uniforms.

"Jonitza," said his mother when she came out, "I am going to call on an old-time friend, and as I know such visits bore you, I shall leave you on the way to spend an hour at the National Museum. How will you like that?"

"Very much, dear mother," Jonitza answered.

So the carriage took them to the big Museum building where Jonitza alighted. Indoors he found much to interest him. He lingered before the displays of magnificent royal jeweled collars and crowns, and the specimens of Roumania's mineral wealth: gold, silver, copper, rock salt, and others. There were drawings and paintings, too, to be looked at. He stood long before one of the latter. It represented a Roumanian boyard or nobleman of long ago, dressed in a long, loose, rich costume, with several jeweled daggers in his embroidered belt. A crowd of dependents surrounded him, some bowing low, some kissing his hand, some trying to get him to listen to the tale that they had to tell.

Although Jonitza's mother was late in returning to the Museum, he had still much to see when she did come. A richly dressed young woman, who treated Jonitza like an old friend, was with her.

"It is still early," his mother remarked to his mystification. And she gave some orders to the coachman who then drove them past the "Institution of the Blind," the particular pride of Queen Elizabeth (Carmen Sylva), past the University and schools of various kinds, past a beautiful pure white marble statue of some voivode or other, and on to the extensive Garden of Cismegiu; then again to the Calea Vittoriei, where the carriage stopped before the renowned restaurant of Capsa.

Here Jonitza's father, who evidently knew of their coming, was waiting to escort them into a room with tiled glistening floor, lofty mirrors, beautiful flowers, and exquisitely neat tables. The place was crowded to overflowing, but above the hum of voices could be heard the fascinating music of a Roumanian Gypsy band.

Hardly had they entered, than two fashionably dressed men joined their party. After considerable banter, the conversation became so serious that Jonitza did not understand all of it. Now and then he caught a quotation that he had heard before, as, "Leave a Hungarian to guard the thing that you value most," and "There is no fruit so bitter as foreigners in the land."

Everything tasted very good, but Jonitza would have enjoyed it more had some attention been paid to him. As it was, he was glad when the party at last arose and while the rest of the company went to the theater, he was sent in the carriage home alone.

At home, he found only servants and so went at once to the little room that was his own during his stay at the capital.

Here he threw himself down for awhile in a big armchair and gave himself up to thoughts that he had never had before, about Roumania's past history, about the old-time ballads of heiduks and chieftains that he had heard in the mountains, and about what he had caught in the conversation at the brilliant restaurant that night regarding Roumania's future.

Even after he lay down on his bed he could not but wonder if Roumania was yet to be a great nation, if Transylvania now belonging to Hungary, if Bukovina now a part of Austria, and perhaps Bessarabia, though claimed by Russia — all with a large Roumanian population, would not be restored to her. Finally he fell into a restless sleep in which he dreamed that he was already a man and fighting that those of his own blood might be rescued from foreign governments who despised them and tyrannized over them.

CHAPTER XV

THE NATIONAL DANCE

When Jonitza awoke he found black coffee and delicious white twists awaiting him. He dressed quickly that he might be in time for the hearty breakfast that follows. It was a holiday, and so later he had a ride behind four horses abreast with his father, first along the sluggish Dimbovitza River on which Bukurest is situated, then into the hills to an old three-towered Cathedral, one of the very few antiquities to be seen in Bukurest. From here the city looked very attractive with its metal plated steeples and cupolas, its many squares and tree-lined avenues.

Then the horses carried them still further away to a neighboring hamlet with its pretty rustic vine-embowered houses, their dark roofs forming verandas on which clay benches invited one to rest. Peasant women drawing water from wells by the wayside greeted them; children tending geese and pigs smiled at them, and a man building a wattled fence invited them into his little country house all blue and white.

When they reached home and had had luncheon, Jonitza found that the whole family but himself had been invited to some entertainment and that he was to be left with Maritza and the servants.

He had begun to yawn and to wonder how he would spend the day, when Maritza solved the problem for him.

"Your mother said that I might take you to see the Hora danced," she announced. The Hora is the Roumanian national dance.

"Oh, good!" cried Jonitza, throwing a book that he was holding up to the ceiling and catching it again.

Soon after, Maritza's brother came for his sister. He was a rather tall, dark-eyed man and dressed in spotless white linen trousers with a ruffle around the ankles and deep pointed pockets in front, embroidered in red. To be sure to be on time they started at once, Maritza laughingly repeating that they "must dance on Sunday to keep the creak out of their bones on Monday."

A half hour's walk brought them to a modest section of Bukurest, where, in a square opposite a tavern, a host of peasant men and women in their gayest costumes, were already gathered. Knowing how eager Maritza was to dance, Jonitza urged her to leave him on the lawn. "I shall be all right here under the trees," he said.

When she consented, he threw himself down to watch. Soon gypsy musicians seated themselves on a platform at one edge of the square and began to play. At once men and maidens clasped hands and began a swaying motion to words improvised by certain of the youths who were in charge of the dance for the day.

Others joined; the ring grew gigantic and then suddenly broke into two, each part with its set of leaders, while a shout of pleasurable excitement rent the air.

Jonitza enjoyed it all for quite a while and then began to yawn. As he turned to see if he could find anything else of interest his glance fell on a boy seated some distance away under a huge lime-tree. Something about this boy made Jonitza sit upright. Suddenly he leaped to his feet, ran wildly forward, and put his hands over the other boy's eyes.

"Guess," he said in a muffled voice.

In answer the other boy jumped up, over-throwing Jonitza as he did so. It was Nicolaia.

For a moment both boys showed considerable emotion. "When did you come? Are you going to stay in Bukurest? Where do you live?" were some of the questions that Jonitza hurled at his companion.

Nicolaia did his best to answer. "I came yesterday," he said, "to begin my apprenticeship with my uncle. Since to-day is Friday and a holiday, Uncle says that I am not to begin work till Monday. He wants me to see a little of the city first."

"Hurrah!" shouted Jonitza, throwing up his cap. "Where are you going to-morrow?"

"In the morning I'm going to go to market with Auntie, so as to know how to buy. I'm to live with them and shall have to do all sorts of odd jobs at times."

Jonitza grew thoughtful. "I'll try to see you there," he said after a pause. "Mother won't let me go alone anywhere here. I'm such a lovely child" — here he grinned — "she thinks some one might steal me. But perhaps I can go with one of the house servants or with Maritza."

"I'll look for you," said Nicolaia solemnly. Then he added: "I was so tired of watching the old dance that I was amusing myself playing Arshitza." Here he stooped to pick up a sheep bone shaped like the figure eight, and some bits of lead.

"What fun we used to have playing that at your house," said Jonitza with something like a sigh. "Let's play it now." Nicolaia nodded and they settled down for a quiet time by themselves, each trying in turn to snap as many of the lead pieces as possible into the rings.

Later they sharpened a few sticks that they found and played another game called Tzurka, not unlike our game of Cat. Then they lay down side by side on the grass and talked.

All this time the music, singing, and dancing went on, as if none of those taking part in it knew what it was to get tired. It was only with the setting of the sun that it came to a stop. Neither of the boys would have known it, however, so absorbed were they in a deep discussion, had not Maritza found them. As she shook hands with Nicolaia and looked at Jonitza's animated face she roguishly asked, "Did you like the dance?"

"Why — yes —" responded Jonitza quite unconscious of the twinkle in her eyes. "It was splendid, wasn't it, Nicolaia? I wish it could have lasted longer!"

CHAPTER XVI

AT THE MARKET

It was not until he was alone with his mother that night that Jonitza mentioned his desire to see Nicolaia at the market on the morrow. His mother put her arms around him. "It is a long time since I've gone to market. Suppose I go to-morrow morning and take you with me?"

"How good a mother is," Jonitza thought as he went to bed, "and how well she understands a boy."

"'WILL YOU NOT LET ME TAKE YOU HOME IN THE CAR?'"

It was delightfully cool next morning when a touring car took them to what seemed a village of booths or stalls, presided over by gypsies, peasants and Jews.

Nicolaia and his aunt were evidently looking out for them for they came up as the carriage stopped. Mrs. Popescu gave Nicolaia a hearty handshake and then turning to his aunt asked for permission to keep the boy with them for the rest of the day. The aunt pointed to a basket over her arm, already filled with the purchases that she had wished Nicolaia to help her make, and cheerfully gave her consent. Then Mrs. Popescu made a gracious offer. "While the boys are enjoying the market together, will you not let me take you home in the car?"

Nicolaia's aunt was evidently surprised and somewhat embarrassed, but when she saw that the offer was sincerely meant, climbed in with her basket, remarking that it was the first time that she had ever been in "one of those things."

As the car drove off, Jonitza grabbed Nicolaia's hand and squeezing it, exclaimed: "Isn't this fine!"

"Bully!" returned Nicolaia. "Let's go from one end of the market to the other."

To show how entirely he intended agreeing with anything that his companion might suggest, Jonitza, laughing, took hold of Nicolaia's arm and pulled him rapidly forward. Both came to a standstill where a heavily bearded man was measuring out rose leaves to be boiled into jam. Near him was a stall with the bright pottery made by the peasants, while across the lane an old woman offered amulets of various kinds for sale. "Buy one of these," she urged the boys as their curious glances fell on her wares. "If not for yourselves, my dears, then for your mothers or sisters; what I have will surely protect them from evil."

The boys paid little attention to her words, but when she laid an arm on Nicolaia he nudged Jonitza with his elbow, said a few words in a low voice and both suddenly darted off, almost knocking down the boys and girls who were going in an opposite direction, carefully balancing stone jars or baskets laden with fruit or vegetables on their heads. They stopped again where food was offered for sale. There were melons and pumpkins, berries, dried fish, caviar, poultry, and bread booths, some of them with women in charge who were knitting or spinning, while waiting for customers.

"Look who is behind me," Nicolaia called out suddenly. Jonitza turned hastily and saw a knife-grinder who, having caught the remark, made a grimace at the boys. They followed him to a booth, and after watching him for a few minutes, made their way to a place near by where all kinds of birds were for sale. "I must have one," said Jonitza, but when Nicolaia could not help him decide whether it should be a parrot or a canary, he decided to postpone the purchase until another day.

This bird stall was not far from another entrance than the one by which they had come. From it they could see numerous carts approaching, some of them drawn by buffaloes, with peasants seated on the front rails.

As the boys eagerly gazed around for anything out of the ordinary, the chant of a minstrel reached them. With difficulty they forced their way into a crowd gathered around an old, half-blind man who seemed to be improvising some fascinating tale of war time deeds accompanying the half-chanted words to a twanging on a flute-like instrument called a cobza. Every once in a while as he stopped the gathered people would shout their applause.

It was not until he grew tired and signified a need for rest that the boys left. Right around the corner they came upon an equal attraction. It was a sort of "Punch and Judy" show to see which a trifling fee was demanded. "We mustn't miss this," Jonitza insisted and led the way into a structure which was crowded with children.

As they came out, a bell tolled the hour. The boys stopped to count the strokes. As they ceased, Nicolaia's face grew serious. It was half an hour past the time when they were to meet Mrs. Popescu. What would she say?

But, when they found her, she did not give them a chance even to offer an excuse. "I know you're late and deserve a scolding, but how dare I scold you when I was ten minutes late myself? I do believe in punctuality, however, for sometimes time is very precious, and I'm going to try not to ever have this happen again. What about yourselves?"

"Oh, we'll try to keep track of time hereafter, dear mother," Jonitza answered both for himself and his friend, at the same time gratefully, pressing one of her hands under the laprobe.

CHAPTER XVII

GOOD-BY

Winter had fully set in when Jonitza and his parents returned to their home city of Galatz. It was intensely cold, for the winds from Russia's vast steppes meet no hindrance in striking the great plains along the lower part of the Danube River. The snow lay heavy on roads and houses, while sprays of icicles hung low from the trees and bushes and even from the noses of toiling cattle. The Danube itself was frozen and would remain so for at least three months. Even the Black Sea further away was ice covered for several miles' distance from shore.

A warm welcome, however, awaited them indoors. The tall brick stove threw out great heat, and the secure double windows treated the powerful wind with scorn.

Friends added the warmth of welcome, and Jonitza was surprised to find how many boys there were of his own age right in his neighborhood. He stared at them as if he had never seen them before and they stared in equal surprise at him. "The fact is," Mr. Popescu confided to the Doctor, "we have brought back a new son."

There was one very bright boy in particular to whom Jonitza was attracted largely because of some physical resemblance to Nicolaia, and this boy's opinion came to have quite an influence over him. For instance when the question of resuming his studies under his former tutor came up, Jonitza objected. "I want to go to the same school as Dimitri," he said. Dimitri was the name of his new friend. "There's a teacher there that knows all sorts of things. Besides, I want to study and work with other boys. How can I tell whether I'm stupid or dull unless I do?"

"I'm afraid I am bringing up a democrat!" his father exclaimed half jokingly when he had given his consent. He had reason to think so in earnest before the winter was over for his son took part in all kinds of sports and picked his associates without regard to the class to which they belonged. Some of Mrs. Popescu's relatives and friends did not hesitate to voice their disapproval. Once they made Mr. Popescu think that he must interfere, but fortunately before he did he ran across his friend the Doctor.

"Your advice has done wonders for our boy," he said to him, "but—" and in a lowered tone he repeated some of the criticisms.

The Doctor gave his cheery laugh. "Let them criticize," he said. "Be thankful that your son acts as a normal boy should act; that he chooses his associates for what they are worth, not for what they can spend. Take my word for it," he added impressively, "class distinctions that have counted so much with some of us, are going to be abolished in our country as well as in many another, and that soon, even if it takes the great war to abolish them."

"SOMETHING CAREFULLY COVERED WITH A SHEET WAS CARRIED MYSTERIOUSLY INTO JONITZA'S ROOM"

Jonitza had made up his mind that Nicolaia must spend the Christmas holidays with them, and Mrs. Popescu was anxious to gratify this wish. But at first it seemed that this would be impossible. It was fortunate perhaps that Mr. Popescu had a business trip to make to Bukurest and so could use a little of his personal influence. That this had some weight was shown when he returned on December 22 accompanied by Nicolaia.

Jonitza had given up all hopes of having his friend with him and so was doubly pleased. He resolved to do everything he could to make the time enjoyable for him, and begged Dimitri's interest and assistance.

"Will your parents let you join me in carol singing?" was Dimitri's first question.

"Mother will, if Nicolaia would like it," replied Jonitza with confidence.

"Then," said Dimitri, "I'll come to your house this afternoon and we'll plan things."

When Dimitri came he was told that Mrs. Popescu had given her consent and the boys retired to a shed to work secretly at the preparations. They were evidently quite elaborate, for Jonitza visited the house for supplies several times. By supper time something carefully covered with a sheet was carried mysteriously into Jonitza's room where a hiding place was found for it.

On Christmas Eve Dimitri was invited over for supper. Maritza herself prepared a special dish called turte for the occasion. This consisted of thin dry wafers of dough covered with honey.

After the meal the boys hurried to Jonitza's room. When they came out it was hard to recognize them. Each had on a mask, a long gown, and a high hat of colored paper.

Nicolaia held a wooden star adorned with little bells. The center of this star was a representation of the manger, and was illuminated from behind.

They took their stand in the hallway where they sang Christmas carols, some of which ended by wishing much prosperity to the household,

"For many years,

For many years."

Then Dimitri led the way to other homes, where he knew they would be welcomed.

Before the Christmas festivities came to an end, Jonitza and Dimitri planned something far more elaborate. It was to act out a peculiar traditional drama for some of the poorest children of the town. Mrs. Popescu lent her assistance and it turned out a great success.

The name of the drama was Irozi, showing that it had something to do with the time of Herod. There were seven boys besides Jonitza, Nicolaia and Dimitri who took part in it. The principal characters were a grumbling Herod, some Roman officers, and three Magi in Oriental costumes, a child, a clown, and an old man.

The plot is quite simple. A Roman officer brings news to Herod (who was impersonated by Jonitza), that three men have been caught going to Bethlehem to adore the new-born Christ. Entering, they hold a long dialogue with Herod, who at last orders them to be cast into prison. They, however, implore God to punish their persecutor. As they do so, strange noises are heard. These frighten Herod who begs forgiveness and lets the men go free.

Later a child comes in and prophesies the future of the Messiah. As the child proceeds, Herod's rage increases until he strikes the child dead. At this all present unite in reproaches until Herod sinks to his knees and implores forgiveness.

The success of the play was largely due to two characters whose antics pleased the little ones. One of these was the clown (Nicolaia) and the other was an old man who was in everybody's way (Dimitri). This latter had a mask with a long beard on his face, a hunched back, and wore heavy boots and a sheepskin mantle with the wool on the outside.

When the much applauded play came to an end, refreshments were passed around and afterwards the children sent home with their hands filled with gifts of various kinds.

In such gayeties the holidays soon passed. On the very last day of the year Nicolaia left for home, and as Jonitza and Dimitri saw him to the train they anticipated the New Year by throwing grains of corn at him and repeating the old time Roumanian greeting:

"May you live and flourish like the trees of the garden and be blessed like them with all things plentiful."

THE END